The Flying Dachshund

by

Debra Menase & Talya Menase

Illustrations by Alexa Gustafson

Published by DM Publications
ISBN: 978-0692178867
Contact: dmenase@gmail.com

This book is dedicated to all doxie lovers and to
Eddie, our loyal friend for sixteen years.

Hi! My name is Eddie.
I'm the neighborhood dog.
Everyone knows me and
waves when I go by.

Wherever I go,
children run up to pet me
and tell me how cute I am.
Some people call me
'the walking hotdog' because
I'm so long and thin.

My long, low shape allows
me to crawl into narrow
places that other dogs can't.
When I turn a corner,
the front half goes first and
then the other half follows.

Sometimes when I have an
itch I have to wiggle on my
back like a worm. I kick my legs
in the air and twist from side to side.
All the kids laugh and say
I look like a belly dancer.

One day, I woke up to the sound
of the wind blowing. I looked
outside at the dark clouds and
realized a big storm was coming.
The leaves were swirling in the air
and the tree branches were
bending in the wind. I really needed
to take my morning walk,
so I thought I'd better do it quickly
before it started to rain.

Not many people were out in this
weather besides the children
on their way to school. They
were wearing their bright yellow
raincoats and rain boots.
They could barely hold onto their
umbrellas. One little boy almost
lost his as he waved good morning
to me. But out into the wind I went!

My ears were really starting
to flap as the storm got closer.
I wished I had worn a hat to
tie them down. I could barely move
as the wind was pushing me
backwards! The stronger the wind,
the harder it was to hold steady.

Before I knew what was
happening, I felt my paws lift
off the ground. Blast off!
To my amazement, I was
actually starting to fly!
I didn't know what to do
but just like an airplane during
take off, I lifted my nose,
tucked in my front paws
and stretched out my hind legs.
Oh, my goodness, I *was* flying!

I was a little worried as
I rocked back and forth like
I was going to roll over
but slowly I got used to it
and I became more steady.
Oops! Bumpity, bump, bump!
I must have hit an air pocket
because my whole body
bounced up and down.

Phew! That was scary
but as I became more
confident and better
at flying, I started to
really enjoy myself.

Wow! I was really having fun
darting in and out of the clouds.
I looked down and heard all
the children shouting in excitement
as they pointed to the sky.
"Look!" they screamed, "it's not a
plane or a bird or superman.
It's Eddie, the flying dachshund!"
I saw the policeman helping
the children cross the street and
the mailman delivering the mail.

The higher up I flew,
the smaller the town
looked beneath me.
Houses looked itty bity.
Cars looked like ladybugs
and people like ants.

It was all going so fast
as I was having a blast.
Finally, I was happy
when my paws safely
touched the ground.

The next morning, my picture made
the front page of the newspaper.
I had become the famous dog known
as *Eddie the Flying Dachshund.*
People started coming from all over
to hopefully catch a glimpse of me.
If they were lucky and it was
a windy day, they might even get
the chance to see me fly!

The End

Made in the USA
Middletown, DE
18 May 2019